Anthony's Big Surprise

NEATE™ Series – Created by Wade Hudson

Anthony's Big Surprise

NEATE™ Series – Created by Wade Hudson

Wade Hudson

SCHOLASTIC INC.

New York Toronto London Auckland Sydney
Mexico City New Delhi Hong Kong Buenos Aires

ISBN 0-439-41304-4

12 11 10 9 8 7 6 5 4 3 2 1   2 3 4 5 6 7/0

Printed in the U.S.A.   40

First Scholastic printing, May 2002

◆ CHAPTER ONE ◆

"I'm home, Mom," Anthony Young yelled as he closed the door behind him. He took his school books into his room and put them on his desk.

Anthony's mother would never tolerate his throwing them on the sofa or on the floor. Patricia Young believed everything should be clean and orderly: throw paper in the garbage: wash the dishes after every meal: hang coats and hats in the closet: put books and school supplies on the desk in your bedroom. But very seldom did she have to remind Anthony to do those things, because he appreciated cleanliness and order as much as she did.

As Anthony headed for the kitchen, he bumped into his mother.

"What time is the game?" Ms. Young asked. "Seven," Anthony answered. "What's for dinner? I want to leave a little early so I can meet Naimah, Liz, and Tayesha."

"We're doing Italian today," said Ms. Young.

"Spaghetti and meatballs. In fact, you can set the table now. Everything is almost ready."

It was Anthony's job to set the table and to wash dishes. He had his responsibilities and his mother had hers. For as long as Anthony could remember it had been just the two of them. Ms. Young wasn't married when Anthony was born. His father was killed while serving in the army in Europe before he was able to marry Patricia Young. Anthony thought about his dad sometimes, wondering how he looked and what he was like.

Ms. Young tried her best to provide Anthony with a good and happy life. After Anthony was born she started working for the *Daily World* newspaper as a receptionist. Now she was a sales manager in the advertising department, and one of the company's most valuable employees.

"Oh, I almost forgot," Ms. Young said as she placed several ears of corn on a dish. "You have a package. It came in the mail this morning."

"A package?" Anthony asked quizzically. "From who?"

"From *whom*?!" corrected his mother.

"From whom?" Anthony repeated, accepting the correction.

"There was no return address on it. It's in the living room on the coffee table."

Anthony hurried into the living room and picked up the large package. It was wrapped in brown paper.

It's not that heavy, Anthony thought. As he began to unwrap the package, Ms. Young walked into the living room. She watched as he pulled the brown paper from around the box.

"I don't know what this could be," Anthony told her.

"Maybe it's from Naimah, Tayesha, Liz, or Eddie," offered Ms. Young.

"But why would they send me a package? It's not my birthday."

Liz, Naimah, Tayesha, and Eddie were Anthony's best friends. They all lived on Mary Street. Sometimes, the kids at school called them the Mary Street crew. But they called themselves NEATE, a name they created by using the first letter of each of their first names.

Anthony folded the brown paper and stared at the box that the paper had covered. He was almost too scared to open it, but he managed to muster enough courage to pry open the flaps.

"There are three sweaters in here," Anthony

said softly to his mother.

He couldn't figure it out. Why would someone send him sweaters? Why wouldn't the person put his or her name on the package? There wasn't a card or note either. Nothing!

"Maybe someone is trying to surprise you," his mother suggested. "It has to be one of your friends. I'm sure you'll find out soon enough."

"But those are expensive sweaters, Mom."

"I know." Anthony's mother was concerned, too. But she didn't want Anthony to know.

"You'd better get something to eat. You'll have to leave for the basketball game soon."

Anthony headed into the dining room. Just as his mother reached the dining room door, the doorbell rang, and she went to answer the door. It was Mrs. Delaney, Eddie's mother.

"Hello, Pat. I'm sorry to barge in on you like this, but I need a favor." Mrs. Delaney talked very fast, and moved almost as fast, too.

"What is it?" Ms. Young asked.

"You know our club is sponsoring a fund-raiser next week. We're trying to get as much publicity as possible. One of the ladies on the publicity committee submitted a press release to the *Daily World* but they haven't done anything with it. I was wondering if you could put a word in for us."

"Oh, sure, I'll be glad to Juanita. But I can't promise anything."

"I know, but they respect you. They'll listen to you."

"I'll do the best I can, Juanita."

"That's good enough for me."

Anthony hurried from the dining room toward the front door.

"Hello, Mrs. Delaney," he spoke.

"Hello, Anthony. You're late for the game aren't you?"

"A little late."

"Did you eat?" Ms. Young asked.

"Yes."

"It couldn't have been much. Not that quickly."

"I'm all right." Anthony dashed out the door.

"I guess everybody is at the game," Mrs. Delaney said. "Floyd must have been the first person at the gym. He's so into basketball, he even makes poor Eddie uncomfortable."

"He's very supportive of Eddie. He's a good father. I know Anthony respects him a lot." Ms. Young sounded a little envious.

"I must admit Floyd is a good father, even if he is a little overbearing."

"Sometimes I wish Anthony had a father around the house. A boy needs a male figure around so he can learn to be a man."

"You have done a great job with Anthony, Pat. You ought to be proud. I think you have done a better job than Floyd and I have done with Eddie and Daisey."

"I've tried my best. But you really never know what a child has missed until later. And then it's too late."

"That's true even for families with a father and a mother, Pat."

"I guess so," Ms. Young told her friend as she walked slowly from the sofa toward the dining room.

"Would you like dinner, Juanita? I'm hungry."

"No, thanks. I've already prepared dinner at home," replied Mrs. Delaney. "In fact, I should get back there now."

Ms. Young escorted Mrs. Delaney to the door.

"See you later, Pat," Mrs. Delaney said as she walked onto the porch.

"O.K.," Ms. Young said. She closed the door gently behind her neighbor.

◆ CHAPTER TWO ◆

Eddie hadn't seen a moment of action in the entire basketball game. He sat on the end of the bench, his face buried in his hands. Every so often, his father would yell, "if you want to win the game, put in Eddie Delaney." But Mr. Delaney only made it worse for Eddie.

"Why doesn't Dad just chill out?" Eddie whispered softly to himself. "He always makes me look bad in front of my friends."

Anthony, Naimah, Liz and Tayesha sat right behind the DuSable Junior High bench.

"It doesn't look like Eddie is gonna get to play in this game either," Anthony told the others.

"Yeah, poor Eddie. I feel sorry for him," chimed in Liz.

"Don't pity him, Liz," cautioned Anthony. "He wouldn't want pity from anybody."

"No, not Eddie," seconded Naimah.

"Maybe basketball is not for him," offered Tayesha.

"Eddie is good. Coach Hamilton just won't give him a chance. He's got an excellent jump shot." Anthony stood up and demonstrated.

Only five minutes remained in the game, now. The DuSable Bulldogs trailed Marshall by eight points. It was a tough game, and Marshall was a good team. But DuSable played hard. Heavy Kyle Lufton, DuSable's star football player, had pushed his muscular body up and down the court, knocking over Marshall players in the process.

"Get him out of the game!" the Marshall coach yelled to the referees after Kyle had run over his point guard. "He's gonna hurt all of my players. This isn't football!"

Heavy Kyle just smiled at the coach.

Hassan Youngblood, the tall, skinny kid from North Carolina blocked five shots with his long arms. And Jimmy Frederick, DuSable's best player, scored a lot of points. He could really shoot. Yes, DuSable was playing well, but Marshall was playing better.

Suddenly, the Bulldogs scored two quick baskets. Hassan blocked a shot and passed the ball to Jimmy who put it in the goal for a basket. Then Jimmy stole a pass and scored another basket.

The DuSable faithful went wild. There was so much noise no one could hear the referee whistle a time out for the Marshall team.

"That's the way to go, Bulldogs! That's the way to go!" yelled the DuSable cheerleaders. The DuSable students joined in, dancing and singing excitedly. The small gym seemed to shake from all the noise.

There were just two minutes left in the game and Marshall lead by four points. Suddenly one of DuSable's players fell to the floor holding his ankle. All of his teammates gathered around him, making the injured player's number 43 jersey barely visible.

"That's Jimmy Frederick," Anthony told Liz, Tayesha, and Naimah. "Without him, we don't have a chance."

"Does it hurt bad, son?" a concerned Coach Hamilton asked Jimmy.

"Yeah, Coach," Jimmy answered with a grimace. He held his ankle as tightly as he could, trying to ease the pain.

"We better have that ankle looked at," said the dejected coach. He would have to finish the game without one of his best players. Several team members helped Jimmy to the bench.

Coach Hamilton pondered for a moment. Who would he use to replace Jimmy? His team still had a chance to win the game. The score was 44-40. He needed someone who could score. As he looked down his team's bench, his eyes fell upon Eddie.

"Delaney!" he yelled. "You're in!"

"Me?!" Eddie couldn't believe what he had heard.

"Yeah, you, Delaney!"

"Yesssss!" yelled Eddie as he thrust a fist into the air. He was so excited he ran onto the court. He had forgotten a time-out had been called and both teams were huddled near their benches.

"What's Eddie doing?" asked Tayesha.

"He's going into the game," explained Anthony. "He's just so excited he doesn't know where he is."

"Poor Eddie," Liz said, shaking her head.

"Liz, Eddie is not a basket case. O.K?!" snapped Naimah.

"All right, girlfriend. I'm just talking."

Coach Hamilton gave his players a few encouraging words as they took the floor again.

"Delaney, stay under control," he told Eddie. "Shoot the jump shot when you get a chance.

Just like you do in practice."

DuSable scored another point on a free throw. The Bulldogs now trailed by three points. Less than a minute remained in the game. A Marshall player intercepted a DuSable pass and headed for the basket. Another two points would put the game out of reach. But as the Marshall forward tried to dribble the ball around Kyle Lufton, the ball hit one of Kyle's huge thighs. Eddie grabbed the loose ball and tossed it to a streaking teammate who missed the shot but was fouled. After the player made one free throw, the score was Marshall 44, DuSable 42.

The Marshall coach called a time-out and instructed his players to just dribble the ball and let the clock run out.

"We're leading," he said. "We don't have to score again."

Coach Hamilton told the Bulldogs to go for a steal.

"If you make a steal, and if there is enough time, go for a lay-up. If there isn't enough time, shoot the jump shot."

All of the students behind the DuSable bench were in a frenzy. Their team actually had a chance to win their first game of the season.

"Let's go, Bulldogs. Let's go! Let's go, Bull-dogs! Let's go!" they chanted.

But, the Marshall team followed their coach's advice perfectly. They passed the ball, and dribbled it as the clock ticked—toward zero. Less than ten seconds now remained. A Marshall player dribbled the ball to the corner of the court. Two DuSable players surrounded him. The Marshall player was trapped. He passed the ball across court toward a teammate. Eddie stepped in front of the teammate, intercepted the ball and dribbled up the court as fast as he could. He looked up at the clock and saw the hand approaching zero.

"Shoot it just like in practice," he told himself. "Shoot it just like in practice."

Eddie held the basketball just above his head, and in one continuous motion launched the ball toward the goal. Just before the buzzer sounded to end the game, the ball nestled softly in the net for a moment and fell to the floor. A three pointer! The final score, DuSable 45, Marshall 44.

The DuSable students ran onto the gym floor. Some were yelling. Some were clapping. Others lifted Eddie off the floor and paraded him around the gymnasium. An excited Mr. Delaney couldn't even reach his son. He ran around the gym yelling, "I told you if you wanted to win the game, put in Eddie Delaney!"

A short while later, Eddie, Naimah, Liz, Anthony, and Tayesha walked home together.

"I've gotta stay away from him," Liz joked Eddie.

"We won't be able to stand you for the next week."

"You mean, I'm gonna be like you were when you won that singing contest?" Eddie shot back. "Not even."

"That was an exciting game," said Naimah.

"I told everybody I could play if I had the chance. Now maybe Pops will buy those new sneakers for me."

The five friends neared Mary Street. Suddenly, Anthony remembered the package. In all of the excitement he had forgotten about it.

"Listen up. You guys aren't playing a trick on me are you?"

"A trick?" asked Naimah curiously.

"Yeah. Someone sent me three sweaters in the mail. There was no card or nothing. I don't know who it's from."

"That's weird," interjected Eddie.

"Yeah, that sure is," seconded Liz.

"Are you guys sure?"

"We wouldn't send you sweaters, man," quipped Eddie. "Be serious. None of us has money like that."

"Yeah," Tayesha agreed. "Well, I have a lot of homework. I have chores to do, too. So, you won't see me anymore until tomorrow."

"Hey, yo. I'm not doing any chores. I'm a star," boasted Eddie.

"Boooooo!" the Naimah, Tayesha, Liz and Anthony chorus sang playfully as the friends made their way down Mary Street.

◆ CHAPTER THREE ◆

The next morning, Anthony hurried to meet Naimah. They had planned to walk to school together. Anthony didn't like to be late. Nor did Naimah. He was afraid she had gone on without him. As Anthony neared Naimah's house, he could see her standing in her yard.

"Sorry, I'm late," he said as he ran up to her.

"We'd better hurry," Naimah said.

As they neared the school, Naimah spotted a man seated in a car. It seemed to her the man was watching them.

"Is that guy staring at us?" Naimah asked Anthony.

"What guy?" Anthony questioned.

"The guy sitting in that blue car parked on the corner."

Anthony turned toward the car but the man was looking in the opposite direction.

"He's not looking at us. He's looking down the street."

"Well, he was when I saw him."

"You're just imagining things, Naimah."

When Anthony and Naimah reached the school, they saw a large group of students gathered on the school lawn. There was a group of black students on one side of the lawn and a group of white students on the other side. A smaller group of Hispanic students stood in the center.

Naimah and Anthony wondered what was going on. A few students usually hung out with students from their own cultural group. Most students, however, were not concerned about each other's background. They were too busy doing the things that students usually do, going to class, having fun, studying. This morning, however, all the white students were together, all of the black students were together and all of the Hispanic students were together.

When Naimah and Anthony reached the lawn, they asked a black student what was going on.

"You didn't hear?" the student asked. "Where have you been?"

The student went on to tell the two friends about the latest news. There was a fight the night before. A group of black students and white students had thrown bottles and rocks at each other following a dance at a local youth center. The dance had been held following the basketball game. A number of students from DuSable were involved. Several of them had been injured, two seriously. Of course, each group blamed the other for the fight.

"We black students got to stick together," the student told Naimah and Anthony.

Just then, the school's new principal, Mr. Epson, came out of the school building and ordered the students to break up and go inside.

All during the school day black and white students stared at each other. Several fights almost broke out. Mr. Epson had to go into one classroom to restore order. During a break, a black student pushed a white student against the wall in the hallway. A white student tripped a black student deliberately.

DuSable Junior High School had an almost equal number of black students and white students. Ten per cent of the student body was Hispanic. There had been racial tensions before, but normally, all of the students got along. This situation was extremely serious. Almost everyone had forgotten about Eddie's winning shot the night before.

"Doesn't anyone remember what I did last night?" Eddie asked Liz rhetorically.

"What do you expect?" Liz replied. "It was just a basketball game."

During a class break, Anthony stopped Naimah in the hallway.

"I think we're in for big trouble unless someone does something. This stuff is serious."

"I think you're right," a concerned Naimah replied. "This is very serious. Even Gloria didn't speak to me today."

"You mean, the white girl who wants to be like you?"

"She doesn't want to be like me. She just likes me, that's all. Anyway, she didn't say one word to me today."

"Well, you're the president of the student council."

"I know that." Naimah pondered for a moment.

"I'm going to talk to Mr. Epson. I think the student council should call an assembly so we can talk about this."

Naimah rushed to the principal's office. Several parents were already meeting with Mr. Epson.

"What's going on?" whispered his secretary to Naimah. "I've never seen the school like this."

Mrs. Sullivan was the nosey type. She had to know what was going on.

"I don't know," answered Naimah. "I heard there was a fight last night among some of our students. I don't know how it started or who started it."

"Black students and white students fighting each other, huh?"

"That's what I heard. That's why I want to talk to Mr. Epson. I think we should have assembly so we can talk about it."

"Those parents are talking with him now. They're really angry. Mr. Epson has already suspended three students."

"Who were they?" asked Naimah. She was surprised to hear that students had already been suspended.

"I'm not supposed to tell anyone. Mr. Epson wouldn't like it if I were to do that."

"We'll find out soon, anyway. You can't keep something that important a secret."

"You're right," Mrs. Sullivan said. "You're so smart. You're just like your mother."

Mrs. Sullivan moved several sheets of papers

as she searched for the one that had the names on it.

"Let's see, here it is right here. Don't you let anybody know I told you."

"I won't," Naimah assured.

"David Williams is one of them," Mrs. Sullivan said. "Tarik Johnson and Sharif Jemison are the other two."

"But they are all black. I thought black and white students were involved in the fight."

"I don't know. Mr. Epson sent those three home thirty minutes ago."

Just then, four white parents exited Mr. Epson's office. He followed them.

"I can assure you that we are on top of everything," Mr. Epson told them as he walked the parents to the door. "You don't have anything to worry about. DuSable will never sink to the level of some of the city's other schools."

"I certainly hope not," one of the parents said pointedly. "I will take my son out of this school." The four parents left.

"Can I help you, Jackson?" Mr. Epson asked as he turned to Naimah.

"Mr. Epson, I think we should have an assembly so students can discuss what's causing the problem here at DuSable. I think an assembly would be a good way to let students express what's on their minds."

"We have already gotten to the bottom of it. We have already suspended the troublemakers. It is always a few who causes problems."

"But Mr. Epson, you only suspended black students. There weren't any white students involved?"

Mr. Epson looked at Naimah.

"How do you know they are black students?" Mrs. Sullivan began to shuffle the papers on her desk, as she glanced sheepishly at Mr. Epson.

"Well..., I saw them." Naimah was always able to think quickly.

"Those three boys are always causing trouble. I think they belong to a gang. We'll soon be back to normal now that they are suspended."

Mr. Epson walked into his office and Naimah followed. The principal kept a neat office. The papers on the desk were in several tidy stacks. The waste paper basket was emptied. The floor had been freshly cleaned.

As Mr. Epson moved toward his desk, he spotted a tissue on the floor near the leg of the desk. He picked up the tissue as if he was afraid it would leap up and bite him. He flung it into the waste paper basket.

"Mr. Epson, this is more serious than you think," protested Naimah. "I think the students really need to talk."

"You're forever the politician, aren't you? Just like your mother."

Mr. Epson sat down in his chair and picked up a writing pen. Naimah just looked at him. True, her mother was a politician, and a good one.

Mrs. Jackson was a member of the city council. But Naimah couldn't understand what her mother had to do with all of this.

Naimah counted to ten slowly. That's what she always did when she felt herself getting angry. Usually it worked. But this Mr. Epson was a challenge. He had made life at DuSable difficult for her ever since he replaced Mr. Maloney, the old principal. Mr. Maloney had to retire because he'd had a heart attack right in his office. Very few students liked Mr. Epson. He had no style. Worse than that, he thought he was a general of an army instead of a school principal. Naimah suspected he didn't like her because he didn't want a black student to be president of the student council.

"I don't think suspending those three black students is going to solve the problem. Black and white students are not speaking to each other. There were a couple of fights this morning during class break. It is serious, Mr. Epson."

"Tomorrow, things will all be normal again. Now, go back to your class. You'll miss the entire session."

Mr. Epson began to shift paper around on his desk. Naimah started to count to ten again, and hurried from the office.

After school, as Naimah, Liz, Tayesha, Eddie, and Anthony walked home, they could feel the tension in the air. Two white students threw a rock and hit a black girl. A group of black students chased them, caught the two and roughed them up. Later, three black students chased a white student for no apparent reason, pelting him with pebbles.

"I wonder how all of this started in the first place?" Anthony wondered out loud.

"I don't know," Naimah responded. "But we definitely have a problem here at DuSable."

◆ CHAPTER FOUR ◆

Anthony was glad to finally get home. It had been a long day and he was really hungry. As he approached the steps of his house he thought he could see a small object near the door. He quickened his pace. When he reached the steps he saw that it was a box. He picked it up and looked at it. There was no return address on it, just like the large box he had gotten the day before.

"What's going on, here?" he asked out loud.

When Anthony's mother returned from work, he showed her the box.

"Did you open it?" she asked.

"No. I wanted to wait until you came."

"Open it. Let's see what it is."

Anthony opened the box. In it was a gold watch. It wasn't a cheap watch with big numbers on the face. This was an expensive watch, the kind that had to be taken to a repair shop if the smallest thing went wrong.

"This is beautiful," Ms. Young said as she stared at the watch. "Someone has to be playing a joke. What else can it be?" She had no other explanation. The watch had to have cost a lot of money.

"Can I wear it?"

"No. Put it up with the sweaters. It has to be a mistake or a prank. I'm sure it's nothing to be concerned about."

But Ms. Young was concerned. Getting presents without knowing who sent them was becoming very scary.

That evening, Eddie, Liz, Tayesha, and Anthony met at Naimah's house. When there was a crisis, the five friends would always meet to find a solution. Naimah had just finished her homework.

"I have to do something about the problem at school," Naimah told the others. "You guys have to help me."

"Let them act silly if they want to," Liz said, somewhat teasingly. She pulled another chip from the bag she held in her hands.

"Be serious, Liz," chastised Naimah.

"Yeah, be serious. At least sometimes." Eddie enjoyed needling Liz. He reached into Liz's bag and pulled out a handful of chips. Liz reached for this hand but it was too late.

"Look who's talking about being serious," Liz shot back. "And you better leave my chips alone."

"Come on you guys. Stop playing around." Naimah picked up the newspaper from her bed.

"See this article in today's paper? Our school is looking bad. And I'm the president of the student council. I'm taking this personally."

"Does the paper say how this started?" Anthony asked.

"It says that a couple of black guys and white guys started a fight the night following the basketball game. It doesn't say why."

"There have been fights before. How did it become such a big racial thing?" Tayesha wanted to know.

"That's what we need to find out," was Naimah's answer.

"Listen, I want you guys to go with me to meet Mr. Epson tomorrow. We have to convince him to call an assembly. I tried to get him to do it today, but he said it wasn't necessary. He thinks because he suspended David, Tarik, and Sharif that everything will be all right. But tomorrow, it's going to be worse. Josh will not let him get away with suspending those students without a fight."

"You can say that again," seconded Tayesha.

Josh Canada was considered by many DuSable students to be the campus militant. He, however, always insisted that he was just making sure that black students at the school were being treated fairly. Whenever he felt a black student was being mistreated he came to that student's rescue. He had five or six supporters who always agreed with him.

Josh often found himself in conflict with Randy Leclair, DuSable's "right wing" leader. Randy had taken the mantle from Pete Russell, who had championed the cause of the conservative students on campus last school year. Pete had transferred to a private school.

"Don't let me down, Randy," Pete had told his friend before he left. "Stand tall!"

"I will," Randy promised. Randy was not as smart or as smooth as Pete, but he tried his best to do what he thought Pete would do in any situation.

"So, what time do you want us to meet you tomorrow?" Anthony asked Naimah.

"Let's meet after second period. I'm going to try to get a few more students to come."

"Well, I'm out of here," said Eddie. "As usual, my Pops has chores for me to do. I bet Michael Jordan doesn't have to do chores."

Liz glared at Eddie. "You are no Michael Jordan."

"It's just a matter of time. I'm getting there." Eddie pretended to dribble a basketball around Liz. As he circled her, he tapped her on the back of the head.

"Stop it, Eddie! Why don't you grow up?!" Eddie ran out the door laughing so hard he nearly fell. Anthony, Liz, and Tayesha followed him.

◆ CHAPTER FIVE ◆

The next day a group of students headed by Naimah waited to meet Mr. Epson. Among the group were Gilbert Perez, president of the United Hispanic Organization on campus; Sarah Bernstein, vice president of the student council; Liz, Anthony, Tayesha, and Eddie.

"Mr. Epson will be with you in a minute," Mrs. Sullivan told the group. She called Naimah to her desk.

"What's going on?" she asked in a whisper.

"We want Mr. Epson to call an assembly so we can talk about the problem."

"He had better do something. He has been getting calls all morning." Suddenly, Mr. Epson appeared.

"You students want to see me?" he asked as he stood just outside his office.

"Yes, Mr. Epson," Naimah answered. She moved from the secretary's desk toward Mr. Epson's office.

"Well, come on in. I don't have much time.

It's a busy day."

The students walked into Mr. Epson's office.

"What do you want?" the principal asked the students as he sat at his desk.

"Mr. Epson, we think you should call an assembly today. The students need an opportunity to share their concerns and to talk about the problem."

"You insist on this assembly, don't you, Jackson?"

"We all think there should be an assembly," Sarah Bernstein jumped in.

"Yes, Mr. Epson, I think we should have one today. It doesn't make much sense for us to not do anything," Gil spoke up.

"Perez, are you saying the administration is not doing anything?" Mr. Epson stared at Gilbert as he stood up from his desk.

"No, Mr. Epson," Gilbert replied undaunted. "We just think the assembly would be another way to deal with the problem we have here. We're scheduled to have an assembly next week, anyway. We can just hold it early."

"I think we can do a lot of good if we talk to the students," Naimah chipped in.

Mr. Epson thought for a moment.

"All right. All right. I'll call for assembly this afternoon following lunch. But I'll address the students myself. This is a very sensitive situation. One wrong word could cause more trouble."

"But, Mr. Epson..."

"That's it, Jackson. Now you students go back to class. I'll see you this afternoon at the assembly." Mr. Epson sat back at his desk again and picked up the telephone. The group of students left his office.

"I can't stand that man," Liz said as they reached the hallway.

"Yeah, where is Mr. Maloney when we need him?" quipped Eddie.

Naimah turned to Sarah and Gilbert.

"Thanks for your help, guys. Let's hope for the best."

Naimah, Liz, Anthony, Tayesha, and Eddie were among the first students in the gymnasium. They watched as most of the white students gathered on one side of the gym while the black students assembled on the other side. The Hispanic students sat toward the back. Before long, the gym was filled.

"Shouldn't you be on stage with Mr. Epson?" Anthony asked Naimah.

"Yes, I should. That's the way Mr. Maloney conducted assembly. Mr. Epson is out of his mind."

"Yeah. Where did he come from?" added Eddie.

The gym was extremely noisy. Some white and black students glared at each other. Naimah spotted Josh and his group.

"I wonder where Randy is?"she asked her friends.

"Over there," Anthony answered, pointing to a circle of white students surrounding a sandy-haired, slender boy. "I see he's holding court."

Mr. Epson walked to the podium and looked out at the sea of students. He adjusted the microphone and cleared his throat.

"May I have your attention!" The noise continued.

"May I have your attention, students!"

"He's going to have to do better than that," joked Eddie. Some of the teachers walked among the students, urging them to be quiet.

"I am not going to ask you anymore. You had better be quiet, now!" Finally the noise subsided.

"Students, I am quite concerned about what has been going on here at the school during the last few days. We will not have students fighting students! That is not the proper environment for the educational process!"

"This guy is a joke," a student seated in front of NEATE said.

"Yeah. A big joke," another student added.

"Now I know that only a few students have been causing the problems," Mr. Epson went on. "We have already addressed that. I am appealing to the rest of you to not let a few students influence you to do wrong. Do I make myself clear?"

Suddenly, Josh stood up. "Mr. Epson, why did you only suspend three black students?" he yelled out.

"Why didn't you suspend the white students, too? They were involved in the fight, too."

Cheers and applauds rang out from the black section of the gym. Naimah looked at Anthony, Eddie, Liz and Tayesha.

Eddie stared at Mr. Epson for a long moment, then shook his head at the nervous principal.

"I suspended those who caused the problem!" Mr. Epson screamed back.

"There were three white students involved in the fight, too! Didn't you know that?" Josh walked closer to the stage.

"I suspended the culprits. And you stop shouting at me, young man!"

Now Randy stood up.

"You want to suspend white students just because three black students were suspended?" he yelled at Josh, pointing his finger at the black student leader.

"Randy, you know there were more students involved in that fight! It wasn't just three black students!"

"Ever since you black students got here, this school has had problems! *You* are the problem!" Some of the white students applauded Randy's statement.

"No, Randy, you are the problem! We are here! We're going to stay here! And there is nothing you can do about it!. This is our school as much as it is yours!" Now the black students applauded vigorously.

"We're in for trouble, girlfriend," Liz told Naimah.

"Yeah, big trouble," added Eddie.

One of Randy's friends started toward the black section. Several black students rushed to meet him. Quickly, Coach Franklin stepped in between them.

"There will be no fighting here!" he warned.

"You understand me?! There will be no fighting here!"

The students stood still. Nobody wanted to tangle with Coach Franklin. He stood 6 feet, 4 inches tall and weighed almost 250 pounds. Coach Franklin was an excellent football player back in the day. Some people said he could have played in the NFL if he hadn't broken his leg.

"Assembly is over," Mr. Epson told the assembled students. "Go back to class." He looked at Naimah seated on the first row with a gigantic frown on his face.

"I know what he is thinking," Naimah whispered underneath her breath. "I told you so."

As Naimah and her friends left the gym, it was quite obvious to them that the problem was worse. Randy stood near the corner of the gym, talking to a growing group of white students. Meanwhile, Josh was talking to a group of black students.

"We have to do something," Naimah said.

Suddenly, Naimah's face lit up. "I got an idea. Why should we allow Randy and Josh to do all the talking? We can talk to the students, too. There are other students here besides us who don't want the school destroyed."

Naimah put a comforting hand on Anthony's shoulder.

"That means work, Anthony," quipped Eddie.

"It always does," seconded Liz.

Naimah ignored them, She was focused on the great idea she had.

"Anthony, go to Gilbert and Sarah and tell them to meet us in that empty classroom in fifteen minutes. It's room number eight. Liz, you get Henrietta Davis and Frank Converse. Tayesha, do you know Howard Jones and Paul Pietrekowski?"

"Yes."

"Bring them, too."

"What about me? Who do I get?" Asked Eddie.

"Get Phil Lombardi and Shanna Martin. I'll see you guys in fifteen minutes."

"But what about class?" Eddie inquired. He almost sounded as if he really cared.

"Don't worry about class," Naimah said.

"Right now, this is what's important. You guys can think of an excuse." Off they went.

◆ CHAPTER SIX ◆

Nearly twenty-five students convened in the empty classroom. Naimah was surprised at the number of students who had come. She had expected only the students she had sent for. Evidently, those students had told others who shared their concern about the problem. There were almost as many white students as there were black students. Several Hispanic students were there, too.

"I'm supposed to be in the library doing research," Henrietta Davis told Howard Jones. "That's what I told the teacher."

"I'm supposed to be meeting with the football coach." Howard told her.

Naimah walked to the front of the class. This was normally the teacher's domain.

"I called this meeting because I am concerned about what's happening here at DuSable, and I think we need to find a solution," Naimah told the students.

"I agree," offered Sarah.

"We can't let students like Randy and Josh take over the school. We've got to make our voices heard."

"How do we do that?" Henrietta Davis asked.

"The same way Randy and Josh do it. We talk to students individually, in groups, any way we can. We can even call them up on the phone."

"What do we say to them?" another student wanted to know.

"I'll answer that," said Gilbert. He stood up. "We tell them that this school belongs to all of us. It does not belong to any one group. We tell them to stand up and claim the school and not to listen to anybody who's trying to destroy it."

"That's right, Gil! This is *our* school!" Phil Lombardi added. All of the students in the room applauded Gilbert's manifesto.

"Let's get busy," said Naimah as if she was leading an army.

As the group prepared to leave, another student stuck his head into the doorway.

"Is Anthony Young here?"

"Yes. That's me," Anthony answered.

"Someone is here to see you in the office."

"Me? Who would want to see me?" he mumbled to himself. "It can't be Mom. She's at work."

As Anthony hurried down the hallway the other students headed back to their respective classes, ready to initiate the plan. When Anthony reached the door leading to the principal's office he stopped.

"I hope nothing has happened to Mom. But that can't be it."

He opened the door and walked inside.

"Is there someone here to see me?" he asked Mrs. Sullivan. She pointed to a man seated on the sofa near the wall. Anthony looked at the man. He didn't seem familiar. The man stood up and approached Anthony. Mrs. Sullivan surveyed him as if she was checking out a new dress to buy.

"You must be Anthony?" the man asked.

"Yes, I'm Anthony. Who are you?"

"Can we step outside in the hallway? the man asked as he watched Mrs. Sullivan still surveying him. Anthony looked him over and pondered for a moment.

"Okay," he said suspiciously.

As Anthony walked to the door, he eyed the man. He was well-dressed. His blue tie matched the color of his suit. His shoes were shinned to perfection. Anthony thought he looked like the models in *Ebony Man* magazine. The stranger opened the door for Anthony.

"Let's walk a few steps down the hall. This seems to be a busy place."

Anthony followed the stranger's suggestion.

Anthony could tell that the man who stood before him was extremely nervous. He fumbled with his hat and tapped his foot. Finally, he looked at Anthony.

"You sure are a big kid. Do you play any sports?"

What kind of question is that? Anthony thought.

"No. I don't play any sport."

"What about music? Do you play an instrument?"

"No." Anthony was getting impatient.

"Look, what do you want with me? Why are you here?"

"This is a friendly visit." The stranger smiled at Anthony.

"Look, sir, I have to get back to class. I don't know you." Anthony started to walk away. The man gasped his arm firmly.

"Wait. Please. This isn't as easy as I thought it would be. Look, I have something to tell you."

The stranger loosened his grip on Anthony's

arm. Then he turned away, trying to muster the courage to tell Anthony what he had planned.

"Has your mother talked to you about your father?"

"About my father? About my father? What about my father?"

Anthony looked directly into the man's eyes.

"Who are you?"

" I'm your father."

"What?!"

"I'm your father."

"You're my father?! You're crazy! My father is dead!"

"Is that what your mother told you?"

Anthony looked into the man's eyes again. Then it hit him.

"You sent those presents, didn't you?!"

"I couldn't think of any other way to give them to you. Did you like them?" The man actually expected an answer. But Anthony was't thinking about presents now. He wanted to know who this man was, and what he was up to.

"Who are you?" he asked for the second time.

" I told you. I'm your father."

"I told you my father is dead! Are you playing some kind of game!?"

"No, Anthony, I'm not playing a game. I am your father. I don't know what your mother has told you, but I'm not dead. I've been close to it, but I'm still here."

The man rolled his hat in his hands nervously. Anthony stared glassy-eyed down the hallway. He couldn't believe what he was hearing.

Suddenly, he turned to face the man. "My father was killed in Europe while he was in the army!"

"I've been living in Europe. But I wasn't in the army, and as you can see I'm not dead. I've been playing a lot of music, though."

"Playing music?"

That got Anthony's attention. His mother had told him many times that his father was an excellent musician. He was the best drummer in his mother's hometown. All of the bands wanted him to play with them. He was that good. In fact, before he had gone into the army, he played with a band called "Galaxy", who many considered to be the best.

"What instrument do you play?" asked Anthony curiously.

"Drums. There aren't too many out there better than Charles Johnson. That's me. You do know my name, don't you?"

Anthony was getting confused. The name was right. The instrument was right. Could this man be his father? If so, that would mean his father wasn't dead. But wait, a family friend could know that much. In fact, anybody could know as much as this stranger knew. But why would anybody who wasn't Anthony's father want to go through all this?

"Wait. I have something to show you," the man told Anthony. He reached into his pocket for his wallet. He opened the wallet and pulled a faded photo from it.

"This is you when you were six months old. You mother sent it to me when I was in Paris." The man extended the photo to Anthony.

"Here. Take a look."

Out of the corner of his eye, Anthony could see the man smiling. It looked like a smile motivated by pride.

What's he smiling for? Anthony thought.

Anthony stared at the photo. A part of him wanted to see if the baby was really him. Another part of him wanted the entire episode to disappear. Should he look at the photo? As he debated whether to accept the photograph, the man stood there and just kept on smiling, just waiting. Should he give this strange man more pleasure by looking at the stupid photo?

Finally, Anthony's curiosity got the best of him. He took the photo.

"That's you...when you were six months old," the man said, still smiling proudly.

Anthony fought back the urge to tell him he had already said that, but he thought better of it.

As soon as Anthony looked at the photo, he knew the baby was him. His mother had a similar photo in her picture album at home. There must have been prints.

"I've held onto that picture," said the man, still smiling.

Can this man be my father? Anthony thought. *But if he is my father, my mom has been lying to me all this time.* That thought sent a chill over his entire body.

Anthony looked at the man again, then gave the photo back to him. He turned and walked slowly away. He didn't feel like hearing any more. Not now!

"Wait, Anthony," the man called. "I just wanted to see you, that's all."

Anthony didn't answer. He walked down the hall, back to his next class.

◆ CHAPTER SEVEN ◆

It seemed as if the school day would never end. There was no way Anthony could concentrate on schoolwork…not after what had happened.

When he got home he headed straight to the coffee table. He looked underneath it. There were several picture albums placed beside each other. Anthony picked up the one on the left. He opened it slowly and turned the pages. There was the photo. It was an exact duplicate of the one the man had…the man who claimed he was his father. Anthony closed the album and put it back.

Slowly, he walked up the steps to his room, then moved gingerly to the dresser near the window. On top were several photographs…a large one of his mother, a photo of himself at grammar school graduation, and a very small photo of a man. He picked up the photo of the man and held it in his hands. Very carefully he brought it closer to him. He wanted a good and sure look.

Yes, the man he had seen at school was the

same man. He didn't have the long hair and beard that he had in the photo, but he was the same person. Anthony replaced the photo and stretched out across his bed.

"Mom lied," he said softly, as if he didn't want to admitt it.

"She lied!" This time he said it more loudly and then banged a fist against the bed. But it did no good. Nothing could make the frustration he felt go away. He lay on his back and stared at the ceiling. Five minutes passed. Ten minutes passed. Fifteen minutes. Finally, he fell asleep.

"Anthony, are you asleep?" His mother 's voice awoke him.

"No, I'm just relaxing."

"Can I come in?"

When Anthony's mother entered the room, he didn't rush to greet her as he usually did.

"What do you want for dinner?" she asked. She was happy to see her son after a long day and she thought it unusual that Anthony hadn't gotten up to greet her.

"I don't know. Whatever you cook is fine."

"Are you studying?"

"I was."

"All right. I'll call you when dinner is ready."

"Mom, did you know my father was here?" Anthony blurted out.

"What?" Ms. Young's body froze as if it where a block of ice. She turned to look at her son.

"He came to my school today. At least the man said he was my father."

Ms. Young walked closer to the bed where Anthony was now sitting.

"Anthony, your father is dead. What are you talking about?"

"Mom, he had my baby picture and everything. And he looks just like the man in the picture on my dresser! You told me that's my father, didn't you? He's the one who sent those gifts."

"Somebody must be playing a game or something. Anthony, your father is dead! He died just after you were born. I don't know who that man was you saw, but he doesn't know what he's talking about. I'm going to prepare dinner." Ms. Young started to leave.

"Mom, my father isn't dead, is he?! You lied to me, didn't you?!"

Anthony's words stopped his mother cold. She stood completely still for a long moment, then walked to the bed and sat next to Anthony.

"What did the man look like?"

"He was kind of tall, and he had a mustache. He wore a blue suit and a blue tie. And his shoes looked like he has just bought them. He said he plays the drums."

"That sounds like Charles all right. I wonder why he came back?"

"So, he is my father?"

"Yes, I think that was Charles...your father." Ms. Young sighed heavily, as if she was releasing all the air her lungs could hold.

"Mom, you lied to me!" Anthony yelled out to his mother. "You told me my father was dead! Why did you tell me that?" He leaped up from the bed and walked up her. The look on his face demanded an answer. Ms. Young had never seen her son so angry before. She reached out to him but he pulled away.

"I thought I could trust you, Mom! I thought I could trust you!"

Anthony rushed out of the room, down the stairs, and went directly to the telephone.

"Tayesha, I gotta talk. I got a big problem. I'll meet you at your house." Anthony rushed every word. Tayesha could tell something was wrong.

"I'll meet you on the porch," she told him.

Just as Anthony hung up the receiver, the doorbell rang. He walked slowly to the door and opened it. It was the man who claimed to be his father. Charles Johnson wore the same blue suit, blue tie and shiny black shoes. His hat still did its dance in his hand just as it had done while standing in the hallway at school. Obviously, he was still quite nervous and uncomfortable.

"We didn't have a chance to finish our talk, Anthony," he said. "You left so suddenly. I hope it's all right to come here like this."

Anthony didn't say anything. Charles Johnson moved a few steps into the house.

"I know this is tough for you. I just hope I get a chance to do a little making up to you. I'm back in the States now. I won't be living here, but I will be in the States permanently. I got tired of living in Europe. I guess you can say I got a little home-sick."

"I don't know why you came here. I have to meet someone," Anthony told the man.

"I won't be long. How's your mother doing?"

"What do you care?!" snapped Anthony.

"Okay, I deserved that. Listen. I know I have no right to impose on you like this. I just want to tell you a few things about me, that's all. Let me do that and I'm out of here."

"For good?"

"Yeah, for good."

"Okay, start talking." Anthony moved quickly to the sofa and dropped down on it.

Charles Johnson looked at Anthony for a long moment.

"You're really in a hurry to get rid of me, huh? Well, here we go." He sat on the sofa on the opposite end from where Anthony sat.

"I have been living in Europe for the past twelve years. I had hoped to become a star there. For a while I lived in Paris, France. Then I moved to Rome, Italy. I played many clubs in Europe, and when recording stars came from the States to play in Rome or Paris, they often hired me as their drummer. I stayed in Europe because many people told me there were great opportunities for musicians. One musician who had just returned from Europe told me I would be a big success. 'As well as you play, man, I know you will make it big.' That's what he told me. It never happened."

"My daddy use to tell me I was too impulsive, that I acted without thinking things through. Most of my life I ignored his descriptions of me. But now, I think that my father was right. I never listened. I rarely listened to anyone. I thought I knew everything. I have made a lot of mistakes in my life. I've done a lot of foolish things."

Mr. Johnson let out a big sigh, got up from the sofa and walked to the mantle. He stared at it for a moment. Anthony just sat motionless on the sofa, waiting for the stranger to finish his monologue.

"I know now that I was wrong to leave you and your mother. I chased after a faint dream. But, the past can't be changed. You have to learn to live with it, and with all of your mistakes and bad choiches. But, I tell you one thing, I am a good drummer. It just takes more than talent to achieve success. My father told me that, too."

As Anthony sat on the sofa, he glanced up at the man who stood before him. *He looks rather handsome*, Anthony thought. *And he doesn't sound like such a bad person*. He began to wonder if he would look like that when he grew up. He certainly wouldn't have a mustache like Charles

Johnson. *That mustache has to go,*" Anthony thought.

Charles Johnson walked closer to Anthony.

"It's important for me to explain things to you, son."

"Don't call me son!" Anthony cautioned tersely. "You have no right."

"But you are ..."

"Don't call me that, all right?!"

"All right. All right," said Charles Johnson relenting.

"Look, Anthony, I just want to establish some contact with you. I don't want to walk into your life and try to be your father. I just want to be able to say hello to you sometimes, to chat a little. I just want to know how you're getting along."

"You never cared about me before!"

"Sometimes it takes a longer time for some people to grow up, to mature."

"Yeah, I guess so," Anthony said as he stood up from the sofa. "Look, I have to go."

"I know how you feel, Anthony."

"You don't know how I feel!" Anthony snapped back. "I was all right until now! Before today, I didn't have a father! And I was all right with that! Now everything is all messed up! I mean, how do I explain you?! I don't want to see you anymore!"

Anthony calmed down again. "I told you I have to go."

"I'm sorry you feel the way you do, Anthony," Charles Johnson said as he fumbled with his hat once again.

"If you happen to change your mind, I'll be at the Harrison Hotel for the next three days. After that I'm going to Los Angeles. I have a job waiting for me there."

The man looked at Anthony one more time before leaving. He could see Anthony looked like him. Anthony had a slender body too. The two even held their heads alike, tilted a little to the left. Anthony's nose looked more like his mother's. But he had his father's ears. Charles Johnson smiled appreciatively as he eyed his son.

"Goodbye," he said finally. Anthony didn't look up. His father tipped his hat to his son then left.

Just as Anthony started to leave, his mother came down stairs. The stains left by her tears were still evident on her face.

"Anthony, are you all right?" she asked. As she looked at her only son she wanted to rush over and hold him in her arms. She had always done her best to protect him. Now, she felt powerless.

"I'm fine," Anthony answered quickly.

"Are you sure?"

"Yes, I'm sure, Mom."

"We have to talk, Anthony. There are some things I have to tell you."

"I have to go over to Tayesha's house. We have a lot of homework." Anthony hurried out of the door.

◆ CHAPTER EIGHT ◆

"What's the big problem?" Tayesha asked as she and Anthony got comfortable on the steps of her house. "It sounded very serious on the phone."

"It is serious."

"Well, are you going to tell me or what?"

"You think my father is dead just like everybody else, right?"

"Yeah. So?"

"It's not true. He's not dead. My mom made it up. She lied, Tay."

"How do you know that?"

"Because my father is in town. He came to school to see me today. And he just left my house."

"You must be very happy!"

"No, I'm not! I'm not happy!" Anthony stretched his legs to the bottom step.

"Why not?"

"Because I'm not interested in seeing him. And because my mother lied to me about him!

Everything is falling apart, Tay. We have been living a big lie. Suppose your mother told you your father was dead?"

"My father lives with us."

"But suppose he didn't and your mother told you he was dead? And then you find out he's not. Wouldn't you be mad, too?"

"I guess so," Tayesha answered.

Anthony picked up a small stick from the bottom step and threw it into the yard.

"It has always been just me and my mom. But now I don't know."

"But she is still your mother, Anthony."

"Yeah, Tay, I know that. But why did she have to lie about my father? You don't lie about something that important."

"She must have had a reason."

"What reason can you have for telling your son his father is dead when his father isn't dead? And listen to me. I'm calling him my father. He hasn't been a father to me. A father is there for his son. He doesn't leave the mother alone. Not a real father! My relatives must have been in on the lie. That's why nobody ever talked about him."

"Anthony, you're being too hard on your mother. I don't know this man who's your father.

But I do know Ms. Young. She is a real nice lady. And she'll do anything in the world for you. Really, I think she has spoiled you."

"She didn't have to lie to me, Tay'."

"Well, Anthony, it seems that you insist on being stubborn. You already have your mind made up. You didn't need to talk to me. I have a lot of home work to do. So, I better go inside. We have a busy day tomorrow, too. We have to help Naimah."

"Good night," Tayesha said and walked inside.

Anthony got up from the steps and started toward his house. He was hoping his mother was asleep or in the kitchen. He didn't want to see her, nor hear what she had to say.

◆ CHAPTER NINE ◆

The following day, Naimah and her group spoke to as many students as possible. Some of the students listened. Others ignored them.

During a class break, Josh and several of his friends approached Naimah in the hallway.

"What are you trying to do?" Josh asked her.

"What are *you* trying to do, Josh?" she retorted.

"I'm looking out for the black students here at DuSable. That's what I'm doing."

"I'm doing that, too, Josh."

"By walking around here with these white kids?"

"Yeah. They are students here, too. I'm the president of the entire student council. That means I'm responsible for all the students."

"You mean, you're not concerned about the black students?"

"Yeah, I'm concerned about black students. I'm black, aren't I? But I'm concerned about other students, too. And I'm concerned about the kind of school we're going to have."

"She's an Uncle Tom, Josh, that's what she is!" one of the students with Josh yelled out.

"I don't care what you say," a confident Naimah responded.

"Yeah, you're an Uncle Tom. Just like in slavery days," continued the heckler.

"Be quiet!" Josh cautioned. "I'm doing the talking."

Josh turned to Naimah.

"Look, I know you're doing what you think is right. But do you think it's fair for Mr. Epson to suspend David, Tarik, and Sharif and not suspend the white students who started the problem?"

"Do you know who the white students are?"

"Mr. Epson knows. But he's not going to suspend them. And I don't think that's right."

"Do you know what happened, Josh?"

"Three white guys threw rocks and hit David with them. But David, Tarik, and Sharif caught the wrong guys. The ones who threw the rocks ran. They were trying to start something. Randy knows. Why don't you ask him? But I tell you what, I'm not going to let David, Tarik, and Sharif take the fall."

Naimah watched as Josh and his followers walked away. She knew Josh had a point. Who were the white guys who had started the fight? Did Mr. Epson know who they were? Did he care?

"Are you going to class?" Anthony asked as he brushed against Naimah.

"Anthony, we have to find out who those white guys were?"

"What white guys?"

"The white guys who started the fight. Josh just told me about it. He said three white boys threw rocks at David. That's how it all began. Apparently, David, Tarik and Sharif beat up the wrong guys."

Anthony didn't feel like dealing with this school crisis. He had problems of his own. But Naimah was his friend. He couldn't let her down. She depended on him more than the other NEATE members. Anthony knew that.

"Well, who saw it? Somebody had to see it," he asked.

"Yeah, somebody had to see it."

On the way to the next class Naimah and Anthony saw Sarah.

"How is it going?" Sarah asked. "What's the response like?"

"Some positive, some not so positive," Naimah answered.

"Same with me," echoed Anthony. "We just have to keep talking."

"Sarah, do you know anything about the fight that started all of this?" Naimah asked.

"No. Not really. All I know is that there were a couple of black guys and white guys fighting each other."

"What happened to the white guys?"

"What do you mean?"

"Why weren't they suspended? Josh raised a good point at that assembly. Only black students were suspended. The white guys who got beat up were not the ones who started the trouble. The guys who started the trouble ran."

"How do you know?"

"Josh told me."

"Josh? Can you trust him?"

"Josh is all right," Anthony interjected. "He just talks too much sometimes."

"We need to find out who those guys were," Naimah said.

"Yeah, we need to find somebody who was there," said Anthony.

Frank Converse walked up. Sarah told him what they had just discussed.

"Randy will not allow anyone who was there to talk," Frank told them.

"Why don't we have another assembly," Sarah suggested. "That assembly we had yesterday was a joke. This time we can conduct it ourselves. And if we handle it right, maybe we can get some students who saw what happened to talk about it. As long as we let Randy keep the white students in his group quiet, we'll never get anyone to tell what really happened."

Naimah shook her head. "Mr. Epson won't let us have an assembly."

"Let's get rid of him," Frank suggested.

"That's an idea," Naimah thought. "If we can get him away from school, we could have our own student assembly."

"I can have my dad invite him to a meeting at his office downtown," Frank offered. "My dad heads the Judson Foundation. He'll keep the old buzzard occupied for a while."

"He's head of the PTA, too, right?" asked Sarah.

"Yeah, that, too," Frank answered. "My dad is cool. He'll keep him busy."

"All right, Frank, call me tonight to let me know what time your father has set the meeting for."

"I'll let you know today. I'm going to call him now and have him call Mr. Epson."

◆ CHAPTER TEN ◆

"I'm over here," Tayesha called to Anthony as he entered the cafeteria. As usual, the cafeteria was noisy. The only time it ever got quiet was when Coach Hamilton came in. The coach had not arrived yet.

The students still separated themselves. White students sat on one side. Black students sat on the other. Anthony made his way to where Tayesha was seated.

"So what do you think, Anthony?" Tayesha asked as Anthony sat down next to her.

"About what?"

"Do you think we'll find those guys who started the trouble?"

"If we get someone who was there to step forward."

"Do you think someone will?"

"We'll find out tomorrow at the assembly. That is if everything goes all right."

"I'm not really hungry," Tayesha said, as she placed her sandwich back into her bag.

"Do you want it?"

"No," Anthony answered. "I'm not hungry either."

Suddenly, the cafeteria got quiet. Anthony and Tayesha looked toward the door. Sure enough, Coach Hamilton had just entered.

"Anthony, have you thought any more about your mom?"

"Yeah."

"And...?"

"Nothing has changed. I just can't get these bad thoughts out of my mind."

"Look, Anthony, I always liked you because you have always been so sensitive. You have always been able to look into things and make the right decision. More than anyone else, you have helped me sort out my problems. Being from a bi-racial family is not easy. But you helped me understand that I have to accept myself. And I'm still working on it. But if you hadn't been here, I don't know what I would have done. I just wish I knew how to help you, now. But one thing I will suggest, you should at least give your mother and father a chance to explain their story, especially your mother. She is a good mother, Anthony. And, she loves you."

"Anthony," Tayesha continued, "remember when you were in the hospital with pneumonia? She stayed there with you. My mom offered to stay so she could get some rest. But your mom refused. She didn't want to leave you. Do I have to tell you more?"

"Tay, you just don't understand!"

"Your mom called my mom last night. She was almost hysterical. She was crying. She said you won't talk to her. She told my mom you mean more to her than anyone or anything in the world. She said she's afraid of losing you. You have to give her a chance, Anthony."

"You think I should, Tayesha? You really think I should?"

"Yes, I do."

Anthony looked at the lunch bag that sat on the table in front of him. His mom had made his favorite sandwich, tuna, for lunch. She always did special things like that for him.

"Mom has been a good parent. She has been my mother and my father. But I just don't understand why she and that man that says he's my father didn't get married."

"Anthony, in spite of everything, you still love her very much."

Anthony thought for a moment.

"Yes, I do."

A loud noise from the hallway caught everyone's attention. All of the students and the teachers rushed to see what was going on. Two male students, one black and the other white, struggled on the hallway floor. Both were trying to throw punches at each other, but neither succeeded very often. Coach Hamilton rushed over and grabbed the two boys, one with each hand. They tried to get away, but it was no use. Coach Hamilton was as strong as he was big. When the boys realized who it was who held them, they stopped struggling.

"I said there will be no fighting at this school. I can't control what you do outside here. But while you're in school you will exercise self-control. Come on, you two are going to the office!"

Coach Hamilton led the two boys away.

"Maybe Coach Hamilton should be the principal," Tayesha told Anthony.

"He would be a lot better than Mr. Epson. Let's go and tell Naimah about the fight."

◆ CHAPTER ELEVEN ◆

Bringggggggggggg!

The bell signalling the first class of the day rang loudly. While students scurried through the hall, rushing to class, Naimah and Frank Converse waited near the school office. They knew Mr. Epson had to leave around 9 o'clock if he planned to make the 9:30 meeting with Frank's father. The other students who had joined Naimah in the cause waited for the signal to go to the various classes to announce the assembly. Most of the teachers felt something had to be done. They supported the students' efforts, all except Mrs. Holloway. She was always difficult.

"Wait until Mr. Epson hears about this," she warned. Several teachers convinced her to keep quiet, at least for a while.

"We better not let Mr. Epson see us," Frank warned Naimah as Naimah peeked around the corner. "He'll suspect something."

Naimah and Frank waited. Every so often one

of them would peek to see if Mr. Epson was leaving. Finally they saw him exit the office and walk down the hallway. He left the building, got into his car and drove off. Naimah and Frank gave the signal for which everyone had been waiting. In a short while, the gym was filled with students.

Everyone was there. Randy sat in front of the white contingent. Josh and his group were there, too. Naimah had Sarah, Frank and Gilbert sit with her on the stage.

As the young leader looked out at her fellow students, she felt a little nervous. *Suppose a fight breaks out*, she thought. *That would be the worse thing in the world.* But when she looked toward the door of the gym, she saw Coach Hamilton standing there with his arms folded.

"Thank goodness," Naimah whispered to herself. Then she breathed a sigh of relief.

"May I have your attention?!" The noisy students could barely hear Naimah.

"May I have your attention?!!!!!"

This time she was heard.

"As you know, I am your elected student council president. It is my responsibility to look out for the interest of all of you. Now there is something that's going on here that concerns all of us. We're too divided. Black students aren't talking to white students, and white students aren't talking to black students. It's causing all kinds of trouble. The situation is out of control. We have never been divided like this. And it's hurting the school."

"It's not our fault!" someone from the white section yelled.

"Who's fault is it?" a student from the black section responded.

Suddenly, students from both sections started calling each other names, and yelling and screaming at each other. Coach Hamilton walked slowly to the front of the gym and stood at attention, his arms still folded. The noise subsided.

"We can't go on like this," Naimah continued. "Now, I know there are a lot of students here who agree with me."

Several students raised their hands. Then several more, until nearly half the students in the gym had raised their hands.

"For those of you who don't know, I'll tell you how all this started. Three white male students threw rocks at David Williams and hit him. David and two of his friends caught the wrong guys and beat them up. Now, they have been suspended by Mr. Epson. But the three white male students who caused the problem in the first place haven't been punished. Now somebody knows who they are. Their names should be given to Mr. Epson, and Mr. Epson should suspend them, too. And that should end all of this silliness."

Frank stood up and walked to the microphone.

"I agree with Naimah," he told the students. "I'm proud to be a Bulldog, and I don't want anyone to make my school look bad. If you know something, you should speak up."

"I know who they are," one white student volunteered.

"I do, too," said another.

Randy stood up and faced the students seated in the white section.

"Wait a minute! You can't do that. Do you know what you're doing? You can't fall for this rhetoric."

"We want a peaceful school, Randy!" a white student yelled from the back.

"Yeah, Randy. I want to graduate so I can go on to high school," said another.

"Will you give Mr. Epson the names of the three who threw the rocks?" Naimah asked the two witnesses.

"I don't know," one of them replied. "I don't want to get anybody in trouble."

"There's already trouble. In fact, you'll cause more trouble if you don't tell the truth." Naimah was very convincing. One of the two students nodded she would name the guilty students.

"I'm not going to be a part of this," Randy said angrily. "I'm leaving. Who's going with me?"

Randy waited at the front for white students to join him. Only a few did.

"You are making as big mistake!" he told the other white students. "You'll see!"

Randy and his followers marched out of the gym to a chorus of boos.

"When Mr. Epson gets back, we are going to give him the names of the three students. Now, let's go back to class, Bulldogs," Naimah said happily.

The students rushed from the gym yelling like they had just won a basketball game. Josh walked to the stage where Naimah was still standing.

He smiled at her.

"You did good," he said. "But let's see what Mr. Epson has to say. "Yeah, you did really good." Josh walked away.

Anthony, Eddie, Liz, Tayesha, Sarah, Gilbert, Frank and the others surrounded Naimah.

"You did it," Gilbert kept saying. He placed his hand on Naimah's shoulder.

"We all did," said Naimah. "Now we got to get those names to Mr. Epson and pressure him to suspend those students."

"He should be back in a little while," Frank said.

"Listen, guys, we still got to keep talking," Gilbert spoke. "We got to keep telling students that we we have to be tolerant of each other."

"You're sure right," Naimah seconded.

"Why don't we all go to Mr. Epson's office and wait for him," Anthony suggested.

"Yeah, that's a cool idea," Eddie said. "That's a way to put pressure on him."

When Mr. Epson got back from the meeting with Frank's father he was greeted by nearly twenty students waiting in the office.

"What is this? What are you students doing

here?" As always, he was in a nasty mood.

"We're here to talk with you, Mr. Epson," explained Naimah.

"About what, Jackson?"

"We know the names of the white students who started that fight the other night," Naimah answered.

"I told you, Jackson, I have suspended the culprits."

"You only suspended some of the culprits, Mr. Epson," Anthony said. "You only suspended the black students."

"What are you trying to say? Are you trying to say I singled out the black students for punishment?"

"We're just saying, Mr. Epson, that we have the names of the white students who were involved." Gilbert looked Mr. Epson right in the eyes.

"These two students saw the entire incident." He pointed out the students to Mr. Epson.

"But I told you I have the students who were responsible."

One of the students who had seen the incident stepped up.

"Mr. Epson, Tom Greenway, Paul Dade, and Ken Larkin threw rocks and hit David Williams with them. They started it. I saw it."

"I saw it, too. That's the way it started," said the other witness.

"You have to punish them, too, Mr. Epson," Sarah told the principal. "We treat everyone fairly at DuSable, don't we?"

"We always have," Mr. Epson responded. The students had him cornered.

"I'll look into it." The nervous principal started to his office.

"Mr. Epson, how did your meeting with my dad go this morning?"

Mr. Epson looked surprised.

"Yeah. You had a meeting with my dad. You know he respects you a lot. He thinks you're doing a good job here at DuSable."

"He does?" Mr. Epson was very interested.

"Yeah. He thinks you're the best principal this school has ever had."

"He said that?!" Mr. Epson smiled, but quickly realized he was being watched. He cleared his throat and started to his office.

"He's full of himself, now," Eddie said. Then

he called to the principal who was now in his office.

"Remember the names of the those students!"

"He better do what's right," Naimah said.

"He will," assured Frank. "He has no choice."

The triumphant students filed out of the office and walked down the hallway.

◆ CHAPTER TWELVE ◆

Ms. Young had left work early. She wanted to cook a nice dinner for Anthony and spend some time with him. She had prepared his favorite dish—meat loaf. She had even cooked a peach pie, which her son loved, too. The table was already set.

When Anthony walked into the house he could smell the meat loaf. He hung his coat in the closet and went upstairs to put his books in his room. Moments later he came back down stairs and went into the kitchen where his mother was.

"I have your favorite today," Ms. Young told her son in a soft voice. She didn't know what his response would be. He had been avoiding her the last few days.

"Yeah, I see."

"It's a special dinner for a special young man."

"I'll wash up," Anthony said.

The two sat at the dinner table as they had done many, many times before.

"How does the meatloaf taste?" Ms. Young asked.

"It's good, Mom, as always."

Ms. Young passed the bowl of rice to her son. "Are you still angry at me?"

"No, I'm not angry anymore."

Ms. Young placed her folk on the table and let out a deep sigh. "Anthony, I have to talk to you."

"You don't have to, Mom."

"I want to, Anthony. I need to. I should have told you the truth a long time ago."

Ms. Young stood up from the table. An anxious look covered her face.

"You know I wanted to be a singer when I was growing up. I told you about that. Well, I was pretty good back in my hometown. I got a job singing with this band on weekends. Your father was a member. He played the drums. We were attracted to each other, and we started dating. But I wasn't the only girl he was seeing. At the time he was seeing quite a few young ladies. Because he was in a popular band, it wasn't difficult for him to find girls who wanted him. Anyway, I got pregnant. I was sixteen. Then the band got a contract to go to Europe. The members went, including your father. He never came back. He did see you before he left, but the truth is,

Anthony, he never loved me. I was a young, stupid teenager who was taken advantage of by a man five years older than me. Of course, I was embarassed. I know my father and mother were, too. You know how people who live in small towns can be. So I convinced my father and mother to let me come to live here with Aunt Blanche. I figured I could get a new start here where no one knew me. And I have been here ever since. I finished high school here, and then I went to secretarial school."

Patricia Young looked as if an enormous weight had been lifted from her shoulders. But there was still more she had to tell. She braced herself again.

"The lie? The big lie?! I started that after I moved here. I was too proud, I guess, to let people know I wasn't married. Aunt Blanche and Uncle Harry went along with the lie. After a while, I guess I started to believe it. That's the story."

"He never wrote you?"

"A couple of times. I sent him a photograph of you when you were six months old. But I never heard from him."

"I guess he didn't care about me, huh?" The thought made Anthony feel very sad.

"But what do I care?," he mumbled as he turned away from his mother.

Ms. Young grabbed her son's hand and pulled him to her. She could see Anthony was fighting back tears. And she understood his pain. She kissed him on the forehead and held his head gently against her chest.

"Anthony, he was young and foolish. But I love you very much! You're the best thing that could have happened to me."

"I love you too, Mom!"

Ms. Young cupped her son's face in her hands and looked into his eyes with the biggest and brightest smile one could ever imagine.

"I think I understand why you did it, Mom," Anthony whispered to her.

"Can you forgive me, son? "

"Yes, Mom."

Ms. Young turned away so Anthony couldn't see the tears in her eyes. But they were happy tears, tears of joy.

"Anthony, whatever decision you make concerning your father will be all right with me. I'll have no problem with whatever you do. I just want you to know that."

"I don't know if I want to see him, Mom. It's

not right for him to just come into my life when he wants to. Where has he been all these years?"

"When he leaves, you may not ever have a chance to see him again. You might regret that later."

"Mom, I think you cooked this dinner to soften me up." Anthony teased. He sat at the table again. His mother joined him.

"Soften you up?"

"Yes."

"Was I softening you up when I cooked that casserole last Thursday?"

"Well, let me see. Maybe you were. Were you trying to get me to do something last Thursday?"

"Young, man, if I want you to do something, I'll just tell you to do it. I'm your mother."

"Sure, Mom." Anthony cut another slice of the meat loaf and put it on his plate. He took a forkful and put it into his mouth.

"Mom..."

"Not with a mouthful of food, Anthony." Everything was back to normal at the Young house.

Anthony finished the piece of meat loaf and turned to his mother.

"Mom, I'll make up my own mind about that man. I have to feel good about whatever I do.

It's not easy. I used to think about having a father. I use to wonder what it would be like. But, now, it just seems like a stranger is trying to force his way into my life, our lives. And I don't like that. You understand, Mom?'

"Yes, I think I do, Anthony."

"Can you pass me the rice?"

"You're really hungry, aren't you?

"Yeah, I guess so."

"Is that problem at school over?"

"I think so. That is if Mr. Epson does the right thing. He's suppose to suspend the white students who started the fight. He's already suspended the black students. You would have been proud of us, Mom. We were great."

"Well, that's good. I just hope everything goes all right. DuSable is a good school."

Anthony placed his fork on his plate and stared at it for a while.

"Mom, I think I'll see that man, my father, before he leaves. What do you think?"

"It's your decision, Anthony. I want you to follow your heart. Whatever decision you make is be find with me."

◆ CHAPTER THIRTEEN ◆

Anthony sat on the sofa, waiting for Charles Johnson to arrive. He had called him several hours before to tell him that he could come over, just for a short visit. Had he done the right thing? Maybe he should have just let him go to California without seeing him again.

Anthony sat thinking as he waited. He didn't have anything his father had ever given to him, except the sweaters and watch he recently thrust upon him. There was just the little photograph that he kept on his dresser to show that he even had a father.

Yeah, Anthony thought, *he just disappeared after I was born. It was like he went to another planet.*

Poor, Mom. He left her stranded. I couldn't do that to anybody. I wouldn't do that to anybody. The thoughts kept racing through Anthony's mind. A knock at the door got his attention. He got up from the sofa and opened the door. It was his father.

This time Charles Johnson wore a gray suit with a matching gray tie. His brown shoes shinned just as the black ones had. He held a hat in his hand, too. This one was gray.

"Hi, Anthony. Can I come in?"

Anthony pulled the door open and let him in.

"Is your mother home?"

"No, she went to the store." Actually, Anthony's mother left the house to give her son an opportunity to talk with his father alone.

"I'm glad you decided to see me again. It would have been hard on me if I had gone to Los Angeles without talking to you again." He sat on the sofa, still holding the gray hat in his hand.

"I would like to get to know you better, Anthony. You are my son, and I think a father and his son should have a relationship. Now, I know it's not going to be easy. I understand that. It's going to take time."

"Did you care for my mother?" For the first time Anthony looked directly in his father's face.

"What?"

"Did you care for my mother?"

"Well, I mean, I was young and I guess I didn't really care about myself. All the things I put myself through, I guess you could say I didn't care too much about my own well being."

"I'm talking about love! Did you love my mother?!" Anthony was now as direct as he could be.

His father looked away before he answered. He could sense that Anthony had a special bond with his mother.

"Son, I'm not going to lie. I didn't. I wasn't capable of loving anybody at that time in my life. I was in my twenties, egotistical and as stupid as I could be."

"Your mother was extremely beautiful. She still is. There were a lot of guys who would have loved to have had her for their girl. For their wife for that matter. No, it wasn't about your mother. It was about me, son. I wasn't a man. In fact, I'm still trying to become one now."

Anthony stared at the photograph of his mother that sat on the mantle above the fireplace. His father looked at the photograph, too, then started to toss his hat from one hand to another.

"You love your mother very much, don't you? I don't blame you. She's special. She has done a great job raising you. You got a right to be proud of her."

Anthony's father moved toward the door.

"I had no right to try to push my way into your life. I won't bother you again." Mr. Johnson finally missed catching the hat that he tossed so often. It fell to the floor. He picked it up and continued to the door. As his father opened the door, Anthony turned toward him.

"Do you have an address in California? Maybe we can write to each other."

Charles Johnson's faced brightened. He turned to face his son.

"You want to do that? Are you sure?"

"Yeah. I don't know how often though."

"I'll give it to you." He pulled a note pad and pen from his coat pocket and jotted down the address. Just as he gave it to Anthony, Ms. Young opened the door. Anthony's mother and father stared at each other for a moment.

"Hi, Pat."

"How are you, Charles." Ms. Young carried a bag of groceries.

"I was just chatting with your son. You have done a great job raising him. He's a good kid. Smart too."

"I've tried to do my best, Charles."

"No, you've done well."

"Let me put these groceries away."

"Well, it was good to see you again. You're still as beautiful as ever."

"Take care of yourself, Charles," Ms. Young said as she walked into the kitchen.

"Yeah, she's still pretty," Charles Johnson said to no one in particular. He turned to his son again.

"Well, Anthony, I'm off to California. I'm excited about corresponding with you. I do want to get to know you."

Anthony's father walked over to his son and extended a hand to him. Anthony hesitated at first, then accepted the invitation. His father's grip was firm and strong. Charles Johnson put his left hand on his son's shoulder, tipped his hat and walked slowly out the door.

"He's gone?" Ms. Young asked her son as she peered in from the dining room.

"Yeah."

She walked further into the room.

"Are you satisfied that you met him again?"

"I am. I guess he's not all bad."

"No one is all bad, Anthony. Isn't there a basketball game today?"

"Oh, yeah! I almost forgot! I better get to the gym! I know Naimah, Tayesha, and Liz are wondering where I am."

"Well, you better get a move on." Anthony kissed his mother on the cheek and dashed out the door.

When he got to the gym, most of the seats were already taken. But he knew his friends had saved one for him. He spotted them behind the DuSable team bench where they always sat.

"We thought something had happened to you, Anthony," Liz yelled to him as Anthony made his way up the steps.

"I had something to do."

"Tom Greenway, Paul Dade and Ken Larkin were suspended," Naimah told him.

"That's good." Anthony replied. "Has the starting lineup been introduced yet?"

"Not yet," Tayesha answered.

Just as Anthony was seated next to his friends, a booming voice came from the speakers that were placed strategically throughout the gymnasium.

"Introducing today's starting lineup – for the DuSable Bulldogs, at guard, Frankie Christopher, and Eddie Delaney."

"He made the starting team!" Anthony yelled excitedly. "He made it!"

NEATE didn't hear the names of the other starters. They stood and cheered wildly for their friend. Eddie winked at them, threw his fist in the air and danced out to center court.

"That's your friend," Liz joked.

"Yeah, that Eddie is some character," said a smiling Anthony.

Tayesha leaned over to Anthony.

"Is everything all right?" she whispered.

Anthony nodded his head and gave his friend an approving smile.

MEET  NEATE™

NAIMAH

ELIZABETH

Naimah is a proud, self-assured thirteen-year-old. A born leader, she enjoys coming up with answers to difficult situations. Everyone says she looks just like her mother, who is a member of city council. Naimah loves the comparison. Naimah's mother has remarried and Naimah is fond of her step-dad. But her little brother Rodney, however, is another story. To her, he is the "human-pest."

Liz just knows she is going to be the next pop superstar. She can sing and has won a number of talent shows, but she tends to overdo it a bit. Liz wears leather suits and other flashy garb her father buys for her. One week, her hair is long and flowing. The next week it is in braids. She is always searching for a new style. But she is a "singer" isn't she?

ANTHONY

TAYESHA

EDDIE

Anthony is very bright and studious. He is smaller than other kids his age, and sometimes that annoys him. Anthony's mother is a single parent and his father has never been around. He feels that he is the man of the house and must take care of his mother. She is, however, very capable of taking care of herself and Anthony. Anthony works hard at everything he does and wants to be a lawyer like Eddie's father.

Tayesha's father is African American and her mother is German. Her parents met when her father, an army veteran, was stationed in Germany. Tayesha is quite sensitive about her interracial background. She has always been aware of the stares her family receives wherever they go. Quick to stand up for the underdog, Tayesha doesn't understand why some people can be so mean and hateful.

Eddie's given name is Martin Edward Delaney but everyone calls him Eddie. He prefers it that way. Eddie's father named him after Dr. Martin Luther King, Jr and never lets him forget it. "You've got to have drive and determination, Eddie, if you want to succeed. You can't be lazy." That's Eddie's father. "Sure, Dad," Eddie is apt to respond. Eddie loves sports, although he is not great at any one of them.

About the Author

Wade Hudson has written a number of
books for young people. Among them
are *AFRO-BETS® Book of Black Heroes
From A to Z, Jamal's Busy Day, Great
Black Heroes: Five Brave Explorers,*
and *AFRO-BETS® Kids I'm Gonna Be.*
He is the editor of *Pass It On: African
American Poetry for Children* and is co-
editor of *In Praise of Our Father and
Our Mothers: A Black Family Treasury
by Outstanding Authors and Artists.* He
and his wife, Cheryl Willis Hudson,
founded Just Us Books.